W9-CSR-516

CESAR CHAVEZ

BY ANNE SCHRAFF

Development: Kent Publishing Services, Inc.

Design and Production: Signature Design Group, Inc.

SADDLEBACK
EDUCATIONAL PUBLISHING
www.sdlback.com

Photo Credits: page 30, Wayne State University Library;
page 41, Library of Congress; page 53, David Bacon;
page 61, courtesy of the United States Post Office

ISBN-13: 978-1-59905-245-8

ISBN-10: 1-59905-245-8

eBook: 978-1-60291-606-7

Printed in Guangzhou, China

0611/CA21100813

15 14 13 12 11 4 5 6 7 8 9

TABLE OF CONTENTS

On November 20, 1960, there was a show on CBS called *Harvest of Shame.* It was about the migrant workers who harvest America's food. The show called attention to the fact that migrant farm workers were poverty-stricken and neglected. They lived in bad housing. They lacked decent pay and health insurance. Often, migrant workers were sprayed with deadly chemicals as they worked in the fields.

Cesar Chavez was a Mexican American farm worker. He was the first person to make changes in the lives of farm workers. Cesar did not have much education or money. Powerful people worked against him. But he managed to help the migrant workers win more economic safety and **dignity**. He did this by leading a nonviolent **revolution**.

Cesar Estrada Chavez was born on March 31, 1927, in Yuma, Arizona. He was the second child of Juana and Librado Chavez. Librado Chavez was thirty-eight when he married Juana Estrada. Librado was working on his father's farm as a rancher at the time.

The Chavez's ranch was in the North Gila Valley in the Arizona desert. Librado worked on the ranch. He also ran three small businesses: a garage, a pool hall, and a candy store.

Librado's father was a migrant worker from Mexico before he got the ranch in Arizona. The family grew sweet Malaga grapes, melons, squash, beans, lettuce, tomatoes, and hot peppers. They also raised chickens, milk cows, and sheep.

Cesar and his younger brother, Richard, were good friends. They both loved to play pool in their free time. Their mother was very religious. She taught them to help the poor.

The Chavez family was not rich. But they had a home and enough to eat. When migrant workers passed through, the Chavez family always tried to help them. Migrant workers often shared the evening meal with the Chavez family.

Juana Chavez also taught her children to avoid fighting. She told them that it always takes two people to start a fight.

She said that there is always a better way to solve problems. Cesar never forgot this lesson.

Cesar and his brothers and sisters had a good life when they were kids. They had many chores, but there was also time for fun. The children swam and fished in the river and flew kites. On Sundays, the whole family climbed into the old family Studebaker and went to the Catholic church in Yuma.

When Cesar was two-years-old, the Great Depression began in the United States. It began when the stock market crashed in 1929. The value of stocks fell quickly. Many people lost their jobs.

People also lost their houses and farms. Many Americans did not have any food. It took time for the hard times to reach everyone. In 1937 hard times came to the Chavez family.

There was a drought and economic depression in Arizona. Very little water ran down the Colorado River. This meant that irrigation ditches ran dry.

Land that once grew healthy crops, now was dry and cracked. People had no crops to sell. The Chavez family could not pay their property taxes.

Librado Chavez went to Yuma and asked for a loan at the bank. The bank would not give him a loan, and he lost all three of his businesses. The Chavez farm was sold at a public auction. Librado, Juana, and their children had to pack all of their things into the Studebaker and leave their home.

The Chavez family had always felt sorry for the homeless migrant workers who went from one field to the next searching for work. Now, they were part of that sad group.

The Chavez family drove west to California. They got to the Imperial Valley and stopped in a migrant camp in Brawley. Cesar saw rows of **rundown** shacks where the migrants lived. Cesar was ten years old, and he had never seen such a difficult place to live.

The migrant workers had to pay two dollars a night to live in one of the shacks. Since the Chavez family had no money, they had to keep going. They pulled off the road when it got dark and slept in the Studebaker.

The next day the Chavez family found a job picking grapes. They were told that they would be paid at the end of the week. The whole family worked all week. But they were not paid as they were promised. There was nothing they could do. Migrant workers had to take whatever was done to them.

They could not afford to pay rent for a migrant shack. Many times, Cesar and his family lived under bridges. When they could not find work, the children gathered mustard greens from the roadside. That was all they had to eat.

Cesar and his brother, Richard, worked with their parents in the fields. Sometimes they found ways to earn extra money, too. One time, the boys collected tinfoil from cigarette, candy, and gum wrappers. They made a huge ball with the tinfoil. They sold the ball to a junk dealer. They were able to buy two sweatshirts and a pair of tennis shoes with the money.

Later, someone told Cesar and his family that pea pickers were needed in Atascadero, California. When they got there, all the fields were already picked. There was no work for them. They moved to Gonzales and lived in a small room above a bar. They worked in the pea fields nearby. In three hours of work, the whole family could make only twenty cents.

When there was less farming work, the Chavez children went to any school that was close by. Cesar went to thirty or forty schools during his childhood. The teachers often thought the migrant children were a problem.

Since the children spent very little time in school, they were always behind in class. The migrant children spoke

Spanish at home. But they were not allowed to speak Spanish in school.

Cesar was often hit with a ruler across his knuckles for speaking Spanish. In some classrooms, the Mexican American children were separated from the other children. This was very difficult for them.

The Chavez family always went to church in Yuma. Now, they did not have a church. Sometimes, a priest would come to the migrant camps on Sunday. He would stand in the back of his pickup truck and say **Mass**. Cesar would often help the priest during Mass. Often, the priest would pass out clothing, food, and toys for the children. The people were always in need of these things.

In California, conditions for the grape pickers were very bad. They worked all day in the hot sun. If they wanted a drink of water, they had to pay a nickel for it.

One night, Cesar's father met with other grape pickers to talk about the bad conditions. They decided to demand better pay and working conditions. If things did not get better, they would go on **strike**. Cesar was only thirteen, but he always listened to the men talking.

Cesar's father went to the owner of the vineyard. He told him that the men would strike if conditions did not get better. The owner said that Librado Chavez was a Communist who wanted to start a revolution. At that time, being called a Communist was very bad.

The owner would not change the conditions or the pay. The workers went on strike. They hoped the owner would worry that his grapes would rot on the vine. They wanted him to agree to make changes.

The workers marched around the vineyard in a **picket line**. The owner brought in new workers to pick his grapes. He hired people called **braceros**. Braceros were workers from Mexico. They were allowed to come to the United States to do work that local people would not do.

The braceros all had very poor families in Mexico. They were desperate for work. They sent their money home to their parents, wives, and children.

The braceros did the work, so the strike was broken. There was no reason for the migrant workers to keep picketing. Librado Chavez and the other workers were fired.

The Chavez family went to San Jose. They lived in a barrio called *Sal si Puedes,* which means "get out if you can." It was a poor neighborhood with a lot of crime.

Farmers were paying one and a half cents a pound for picked cherries. After the cherry harvest was over, there was the apricot harvest. Once the apricots were picked, they were pitted and cut in half. They then were laid on drying tables in the sun. The Chavez family made thirty cents a day picking apricots.

Later, in Oxnard, California, Cesar and his family harvested walnuts. Cesar and Richard slept outside in the open. The younger children slept in an eight-foot-long tent. In the winter, cold winds blew in from the ocean. The children's shoes rotted from the cold.

CHAPTER 3

In 1942 Librado Chavez was injured in a car accident. He could not work for awhile. Cesar was fifteen-years-old. He finished seventh grade, but he now had to quit school. He had to earn money for the family. Cesar traveled as a migrant worker by himself.

He went to fields around the state, following the crops. He worked in fields of lettuce and sugar beets. Since he had to use a short handled hoe, he was always bent over. Cesar had constant backaches. Then, he followed the onion planting season. Again, he had to bend over all day. He dug his fingers into the ground and planted the onion seedlings.

World War II had started. All over America, young men were joining the military. In 1944 seventeen-year-old Cesar Chavez signed up for the United States Navy. He became a deck hand on a ship.

By this time, Librado Chavez could work again. There were many men off fighting in the war, so it was easier for the Chavez family to get farm work. The pay improved as well.

The Chavez family was living in Delano at that time. Cesar Chavez started to notice a lot of **discrimination** against Mexicans. Many restaurants would not serve Mexicans.

One time, Chavez walked into a movie theater. He sat down in the section for white people. One of the people who worked at the theater told him to go to the section for African Americans, Filipinos, and Mexicans. Chavez would not move, so the police were called. The police officer gave Chavez a strong warning for his actions.

Cesar met Helen Fabela at an ice cream store in Delano. They liked each other very much. In 1946 Cesar left the navy. Then, he and Helen began to date seriously.

Cesar was five feet six inches tall, and he weighed 135 pounds. He looked older than he was because of so many years of hard work. He had little education, so he could only get farm work. He worked hard and started to save money for his marriage.

In 1948 Cesar Chavez married Helen Fabela. On their honeymoon, they visited all of the **missions** of California. Then, they went back to Delano. They rented a one-room shack with no electricity and no running water. The only heat came from a small camping stove. The couple did not have a car, so they had to ask for rides everywhere.

Cesar and Helen Chavez picked grapes and lettuce in the summer. In the winter, they picked cotton. Soon, Helen was pregnant with their first baby. Only Cesar worked in the fields then.

On February 20, 1949, Fernando was born. Cesar Chavez was making more money, and in 1950, their daughter Sylvia was born. Next, came Linda in 1951.

Chavez and his brother, Richard, rented a small farm in Greenfield,

California. There, they tried to grow strawberries. The two men remembered that their father and grandfather farmed their own land in Arizona. They wanted that better life for their families. But the strawberry farm did not work out. Chavez went back to picking beans for a dollar to a dollar and a half per hour. Two more children were born, Eloise in 1952 and Ana in 1953.

The Chavez family returned to San Jose. There, Cesar met Father Donald McDonnell, who had a strong impact on his life. Cesar and the priest talked about farm work and the problems of the migrants. Because of Father McDonnell, Chavez began to read books about St. Francis of Assisi, the gentle saint.

He also read about Mahatma Gandhi. Gandhi was a Hindu man who helped bring independence to India. Chavez found the same nonviolent message in these books that his mother taught him. Chavez was very interested to learn how much people could do using peaceful ways.

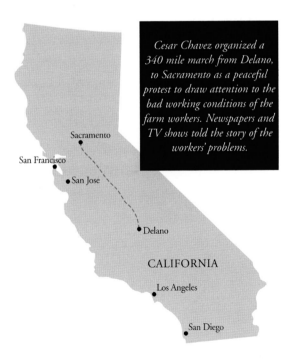

Cesar Chavez organized a 340 mile march from Delano, to Sacramento as a peaceful protest to draw attention to the bad working conditions of the farm workers. Newspapers and TV shows told the story of the workers' problems.

CHAPTER 4

Cesar Chavez then met a man who changed his life. Fred Ross was an **Anglo** social worker. He worked for President Franklin Roosevelt's Farm Security Administration. His job was to organize food distribution, like beans and flour, to poor people.

Ross wanted to do more. He wanted to help people rise from poverty. He wanted to help the poor to help themselves. But he was working in the

Mexican American neighborhoods in San Jose. Ross needed a strong, smart Mexican leader to bring his program to the people.

Ross started the Community Service Organization (CSO). He started to search for a Mexican leader who could help him talk to the people. Then, he met Cesar Chavez. He asked Chavez if he could get a group of his friends together at his house. Ross wanted to come speak to them about the CSO. Chavez agreed, but he and his friends were very **suspicious** of Ross.

Often, Anglo men came into the barrio with ideas that ended up being worthless. When Ross got up to speak, many complained and were not interested. But slowly, the men began to like Ross's message. The CSO seemed to be a good thing. They were trying to register Mexican American voters. When the elections came, the Mexican Americans would have some say in who was elected. An election was coming in 1952. The CSO hoped the people elected would be interested in the needs of the poor.

Ross hired Cesar Chavez as a **recruiter** for the CSO. Chavez went from house to house in the neighborhood registering his neighbors. With Chavez's help, six thousand new voters were registered.

Now, Ross asked Chavez to take on more responsibility. He wanted him to be an organizer. He asked Chavez to lead meetings. Chavez was only twenty-five and he was very nervous about getting up in front of a group of people and telling them what needed to be done. Some of them were old enough to be his parents.

Chavez held back his fear and gave his first CSO meeting in Oakland, California. Chavez was surprised to find that the crowd was very interested. They showed him a lot of respect.

Cesar Chavez was now earning $58.00 a week as an organizer. He traveled all over California, from Bakersfield to Oxnard. He was recruiting people for CSO. In 1957 his son, Paul, was born. Then, in 1958 Anthony and Elizabeth were born. There were now eight children in the family.

One of the first problems that Cesar Chavez dealt with was the lack of farm jobs in Oxnard. Whenever farm workers were needed, the local farm workers were turned away. Instead, the farmers hired the braceros from Mexico. It was illegal to hire braceros if local workers were available, but the law was broken.

On January 15, 1959, Chavez organized a protest march of 1,500 farm workers. The workers demanded they be given a chance to fill the jobs in Oxnard. The growers preferred braceros because no matter how bad the working conditions were, they never complained. They were afraid that they would be sent back to Mexico. If they were sent back, they could not help their families by sending money home. So, they would put up with the injustice in silence.

The U.S. Secretary of Labor, James Mitchell, came to Oxnard to talk to the local business people. Chavez organized a march of ten thousand people to get his attention. They marched behind the banner of Our Lady of Guadalupe, a very sacred symbol for Mexican American people.

The marchers sang hymns and carried signs demanding justice. The marchers had no police permit. But there were so many of them that the police did not even try to make arrests. It was a very peaceful demonstration.

After thirteen months of struggle, the Oxnard growers finally gave in and agreed to hire local farm workers. It was Cesar Chavez's first big labor victory. It had been a hard year. Chavez worked so hard that he lost twenty-five pounds off his already thin body. Chavez was now earning $150 a week plus expenses as a national CSO director. But he had a bigger dream. He wanted to form a union just for farm workers.

CHAPTER 5

Cesar Chavez talked to the CSO directors about his farm union. Since they were not interested, he resigned. In 1962 Chavez had saved $1,200. With Helen's help and her family's support, he believed he could launch the Farm Workers Labor Union.

Chavez drew a map of every town and migrant camp in the San Joaquin Valley. There were 86 in all. He planned to visit each one of them to recruit workers for his union, the National Farm Workers Association (NFWA).

He set up headquarters in his garage. He loaded his Mercury station wagon with sign up sheets. He took his son, Anthony, on some of the trips because there was nobody to leave the boy with. Helen Chavez was working.

Sometimes, Chavez actually went from door to door and to gathering places where migrant workers could be found. Right away, he recruited a spirited young woman, Dolores Huerta. She deeply believed in the principles of justice. She had worked at the CSO with Chavez. She believed in his cause and became a strong force in the union.

Even the Chavez children were recruited to help in the early days. After school on Friday, they would pile into the Mercury. Their arms were full of leaflets that their mother had run off the night before on an old **mimeograph** machine. The older children also helped earn money for the family. They went with their mother to the fields to pick cotton, walnuts, peas, and table grapes. This way, their father had time to organize the union.

Dolores Huerta signs up workers to join the union.

By the fall of 1962, one thousand farm workers had joined the union. Chavez decided there were enough members to hold a convention in Fresno, California. In Fresno, the union flag was unveiled.

Chavez had put a lot of thought into the flag. He wanted it to be simple so that farm workers could easily copy it to make their own posters and flags. So, he chose the sacred Aztec bird, the eagle, and drew it in straight lines. The black eagle was on a white circle and the rest of the flag was red. The black eagle was a symbol of the troubles the farm workers had endured. White stood for hope. Red was for the struggle for justice. The **motto** of the union was "Viva la Causa" or long live the cause.

Union dues were $3.50 a month. Benefits to the workers included a credit bank that would loan money at low interest. There was also a burial society that would cover the funeral expenses of poor workers. Chavez also set up a co-operative grocery store and gas station that sold things at lower prices. Cesar Chavez's salary as union president was $35.00 a week, which included his wife's bookkeeping services.

Chavez also started a union newspaper, *El Malcriado*. *El malcriado* means "the brat," and the paper cried out against injustices. Cesar Chavez's first big challenge was with the grape growers of Delano, California. Grape workers there earned about a dollar an hour. Their average yearly income was $1,500.

At the time, the poverty level in the United States had been set at $3,000 a year for a family. On many grape ranches, there were no toilets in the fields. Workers had to pay for drinking water. Dangerous chemicals were frequently sprayed on the vineyards while workers were present. This created great risks to their health.

The AFL-CIO already had an agricultural union called the Agricultural Workers of California. They were fighting for the rights of Filipino workers. Filipino farm worker, Larry Itliong, was trying to organize his fellow Filipinos to get better working conditions.

He called a strike in September 1965. But the growers found some Mexican workers to break the strike. So, Itliong talked to Cesar Chavez. Chavez's union voted to join Itliong's cause. Then, Filipino and Mexican farm workers stood side by side.

On the first day of the strike, 1,200 workers walked out from the vineyard. They formed picket lines on the roads leading into the grape farm. Some growers turned to violence. They pointed shotguns at the strikers. They knocked some of them to the ground and set fire to their picket signs.

The growers roared down the dirt roads in trucks. They showered picketers with gravel and dirt. Some growers even intentionally shot fertilizer and insecticides from spraying machines at the strikers.

The police and sheriffs in the area usually sided with the growers. Although the farm union was nonviolent, their members were arrested for various reasons. Dolores Huerta was arrested twice in one week and charged with trespassing. Chavez and a Catholic priest flew over the vineyard in a private plane. When they landed, they were arrested and charged with violating the air space of the grower. Cesar Chavez insisted on complete nonviolence no matter what happened.

To keep the strikers going without their paychecks, Chavez raised money at rallies around California. He appeared at the University of California, Berkeley. The college students donated generously. Help came from many different sources. One dairy donated a hundred dozen eggs a week. A meat packing plant gave forty pounds of hamburger each Saturday. Bakeries donated day-old bread and rolls.

However, the grape strike was not succeeding. The farm workers needed another weapon. That weapon was a boycott of grapes.

CHAPTER 6

Cesar Chavez's farm workers picketed the docks where grapes were loaded for shipment to other countries. The UFW asked people all over California and the United States to stop buying grapes until the growers accepted the union's demands.

In 1965 Chavez focused attention on Schenley Industries, which had 3,350 acres of grapes in Delano. Chavez used a "divide and conquer" strategy. He targeted one grower at a time. In December 1965 the AFL-CIO officially

endorsed the grape strike. It made a large donation to the workers' strike fund.

In March 1966 the United States Senate Subcommittee investigated the grape strike and held hearings in Delano. Senator Robert Kennedy of New York was a member of the subcommittee. He was very sympathetic to Chavez. During the hearings, Chavez and Kennedy became close friends

At this time, a farm worker's march to Sacramento began. The marchers asked for passage of a law to guarantee fair farm labor wages. The group marched behind American and Mexican flags, the banner of Our Lady of Guadalupe, and the UFW eagle. They covered 21 miles the first day. Chavez's ankle was badly swollen. He had a large blister on his foot. By the second day, Chavez's right leg was swollen to his knee. He had to ride in the station wagon.

As the march passed through towns and cities, the marchers were greeted by sympathizers playing guitars and accordions. By the ninth day, Chavez could walk again with the help of a cane. The marchers were treated to lunch by the mayor of Fresno. In Stockton, five thousand people cheered them. At that time, Chavez received a phone call from Schenley Industries recognizing the union and agreeing to terms.

It was raining on Easter Sunday as the marchers got together in Sacramento. Chavez told the 10,000 who came to welcome the marchers that a historic agreement had been reached with Schenley Industries. With the exception of a pineapple workers contract made earlier, this was the first American farm workers contract in U.S. history.

The next target of the UFW was the DiGiorgio Corporation's 4,400 acre vineyard in Sierra Vista. DiGiorgio was well known for breaking strikes. They had broken them in the 1930s, 40s, and 60s. They had strong political influence in the state.

Now, DiGiorgio agreed to talk to the UFW and to hold elections among their farm workers. But the Teamsters were also trying to recruit farm workers. The Teamsters was another union that represented workers in the area at the time. DiGiorgio was sure that the Teamsters would win. DiGiorgio wanted to work with the Teamsters because they thought they would get a better agreement from them.

CHAPTER 7

Cesar Chavez merged his United Farm workers with the AWOC. The new name for the union was United Farm Workers of California (UFWOC). The election began among the farm workers. They were asked to choose which union they wanted to represent them.

At the same time, DiGiorgio got a court order against Chavez for picketing. The Teamsters intimidated some of the farm workers to try to gain their votes. But, when the votes were counted, the UFWOC won by a wide margin.

Cesar with his wife, Helen, at his side, began negotiating with the grape growers for better wages and working conditions for the union members.

In August 1967 Cesar Chavez began a **fast** to affirm the nonviolent nature of his struggle. Some of the younger members of the UFW were getting impatient. They wanted more aggressive measures. But Chavez insisted on the way of peace.

The grape strike was now known all over America. Many people boycotted grapes as a matter of **conscience**. If people did not see the emblem of the black eagle on a box of grapes, they refused to buy it. The eagle symbol meant that the grower had come to terms with the UFW union.

One by one, the grape growers were making deals with Chavez. On July 17, 1970, the big break came. Twenty-three growers were ready to negotiate. They grew almost half of all the grapes in California.

Negotiations were held at the Holiday Inn in Bakersfield. The growers agreed to hire union workers, protect the workers against pesticides, and raise wages to $1.80 an hour. The grape strike ended. It was a huge victory for Chavez and his union.

Now, Cesar Chavez turned his attention to another group of farm workers, the lettuce pickers of Salinas, California. The Teamsters were already making a lot of progress with the lettuce workers. At the end of July 1970, Chavez held a large rally in Salinas. He argued that the Teamsters were not getting good contracts for the workers. The UFWOC could do better. Fights broke out between UFWOC workers and Teamsters.

In August 1970 Chavez called for a nationwide boycott of Chiquita bananas, which were marketed by a large lettuce grower. The same day, the company asked for negotiations. Chavez was able to get good terms for the lettuce pickers. The Teamsters struck back, and UFWOC workers were threatened with baseball bats and chains. The windshields of their cars were broken.

Chavez was ordered by the court to end his lettuce boycott against the growers. But the growers would not agree to the terms of the negotiation, so he refused to end the boycott. He was arrested. At his December hearing, two thousand workers marched around the courthouse praying and carrying candles. Chavez was ordered to remain in jail until he agreed to end the lettuce boycott.

CHAPTER 8

Cesar Chavez's farm workers made a makeshift shrine in a pickup truck across the street from the jail where Chavez was being held. Many famous civil rights leaders came to visit Chavez and to offer their support for his cause. Coretta Scott King came to pray with Chavez. She was the widow of Dr. Martin Luther King Jr., who was assassinated in 1968. Ethel Kennedy, widow of Senator Robert Kennedy, who was also assassinated in 1968, paid her respects to the jailed Chavez.

Twenty days later, the California Supreme Court ordered the release of Chavez. They said he had the right to conduct the lettuce boycott as part of his free speech rights. But talks with the lettuce growers broke down. Although Chavez continued to fight to establish his union in the lettuce fields, the Teamsters were too strong. Cesar Chavez did not have the success in the lettuce fields that he had in the grape vineyards.

In 1972 anti-union forces in California got an issue on the ballot that would ban the boycott and many other effective labor weapons. Proposition 22 was widely promoted before the election. Chavez started a large campaign to defeat it. Proposition 22 went down to defeat 58 percent to 42 percent.

In May 1972 a similar anti-union initiative was passed in Arizona. Cesar Chavez moved into a Phoenix barrio to begin a 24-day fast. His health was poor during the fast. He suffered from an irregular heartbeat, but he would not stop.

Chavez called for a recall of the politicians who led the fight to pass an anti-union law. His target was primarily Republican governor, Jack Williams. Chavez failed to unseat the governor. But his campaign registered many new Mexican American voters. In 1974 a governor more favorable to unions was elected.

In August 1975 California got a new governor, Edmund G. Brown Jr. He was a young, pro-union politician. He put through the Agricultural Labor Relations Act. The act was the first bill of rights for farm workers ever enacted in the United States. Up until this time, farm workers were not given most of the worker protections that covered people in other industries.

In a statewide election of California farm workers, the UFWOC was chosen over the Teamsters, 53 percent to 30 percent. In March 1977 the **rivalry** between the UFWOC and the Teamsters ended. The UFWOC would represent all workers whose employers were engaged in farming.

The UFWOC under Cesar Chavez made some amazing progress by 1980. In late 1960, farm workers were lucky to be earning $2.00 an hour. By 1980, the minimum wage for farm workers was $5.00 an hour plus other benefits. By 1984, UFWOC members were earning $7.00 an hour.

Cesar Chavez was still disappointed by the continued use of pesticides in the fields of California. He also disliked the living conditions for farm workers in some camps. He began another fast in July 1988. He was now sixty-one-years-old and frail.

Chavez described the fast as a way to clean his own body and soul so he could continue helping his people. He also fasted to call attention to some farm workers sickened by careless use of pesticides. Chavez pledged solidarity with the weak and helpless against the proud and the powerful.

The fast was completed on August 21, after thirty-six days. Many ordinary and important people visited Chavez during the fast. When he finally ate again, Rev. Jesse Jackson, actors Danny Glover, Martin Sheen, and Edward Olmos joined with Congressman Peter Chacon to break bread with him. Ethel Kennedy and several of her children also came.

During this time, Cesar Chavez was alarmed about the health hazards of pesticides for farm workers. But, he also worried about how much of it was getting into the food chain. He called it a "crisis of safety."

CHAPTER 9

As Cesar Chavez's health got worse, his daughter, Linda, became very active in the UFWOC union. She was married in 1974 to Arturo Rodriguez, who was working for the union. Over the next decades, Linda Chavez Rodriguez and her husband traveled throughout California and the nation. They were carrying out her father's cause.

In 1993 Cesar Chavez was called to Yuma, Arizona, to help UFWOC workers defend a lawsuit stemming from the lettuce boycott. Lettuce and vegetable grower Bruce Church, Inc. demanded the union pay large sums of money because of the money they lost during the boycott.

The lawsuit asked for millions of dollars in damages. Bruce Church, Inc. could have filed in California. But they felt they had a better chance for success filing in Arizona. The political climate was less sympathetic to unions there.

Chavez testified at the trial, looking tired and overworked. He argued that the lettuce boycott was declared legal by the California Supreme Court. After making his court appearance, Chavez drove through the neighborhoods of Yuma where he lived as a boy. During the happy days of his early childhood, his family often drove into Yuma to go to church and shop. Now, he revived old family ties and friendships.

Cesar Chavez stayed with a family in San Luis, Arizona, about twenty miles from Yuma. After his round of visiting, he returned to the concrete block home in the barrio. At 9 p.m., Chavez had dinner. He then told his hosts he was exhausted from the long questioning on the witness stand in court.

Life in the barrio was hard. The workers lived in small, crowded houses that were often shacks with no running water.

So much was at stake. The UFWOC union was not wealthy. An award against it for millions of dollars would be devastating. Cesar Chavez was always willing to sacrifice himself for the union that he believed in so strongly.

Chavez went to bed between 10 and 10:30 p.m. that night. He was reading a book about Native Americans. The book talked about how they were trying to market the products they made on the reservations. Chavez sympathized with them. They, like the farm workers he had defended, were often stuck in poverty.

A union staff member who was also staying at the house in San Luis saw that the light in Chavez's bedroom stayed on into the night. He thought Chavez was doing what he often did, reading half the night.

Although Chavez had a poor education as a child, as a man, he loved reading. The walls of his office were filled with bookshelves. He had books on philosophy, economics, labor problems, and biographies of men he admired, like Gandhi and the Kennedys.

Cesar Chavez always woke up early. He was usually out of bed by dawn to write or meditate. But, on the morning of Friday, April 23, he did not come out of the room. When union friends went to investigate, they found that Chavez had died during the night.

Chavez had never undressed, although he had taken off his shoes. He was lying on his back with an open book on Native American crafts on his chest. The book was open to the page he had apparently been reading last. He seemed to have died peacefully because any spasm would have sent the book to the floor. Those who looked at Chavez said he had a contented smile on his face.

On April 29, 1993, Cesar Chavez's body arrived at the memorial park in Delano, California. That was where the funeral service was conducted. Fifty thousand people waited to pay their respects. They came from all corners of the United States, by plane, train, and car. Some of those present marched with Chavez on the road to Sacramento or in picket lines. Some had stood beside him picking walnuts, grapes, and cotton.

CHAPTER 10

Pope John Paul II sent a statement of **condolence** and celebration of the life of Cesar Chavez. Cardinal Roger M. Mahoney of Los Angeles called Chavez a prophet for the farm workers. Dignitaries and rough-looking farm workers stood together to honor Chavez. Chavez's body lay in a simple pine coffin. The pallbearers were his children, grandchildren, and people who worked with him in the fields and in the forming of the union.

The funeral Mass was celebrated. Then, the body of Chavez was taken to the headquarters of the UFWOC union at the field office called "Forty Acres." Chavez was buried near a bed of roses in front of his office.

Arturo Rodriguez, husband of Linda Chavez, became president of the UFWOC union. On August 8, 1994, President Bill Clinton presented Helen Chavez with the Medal of Freedom. It was awarded after her husband's death. It is America's highest civilian honor.

Clinton praised Chavez for his nonviolent struggle to gain decent working conditions for the farm workers. Clinton described him as a "Moses figure." He said that Chavez had nobly and courageously led his people to a better place.

Cesar Chavez's lifestyle never changed even when he became a public figure. He never earned much money. During the entire grape strike, he and his wife and eight children lived in a rundown two bedroom, one bath, wood frame house in Delano. His enemies thought that surely the Chavez family had big bank accounts or a fine home. But this was not true.

The lawsuit from Bruce Church, Inc., which brought Chavez back to Arizona in the days before his death, was eventually thrown out of court. In May 1996 Bruce Church, Inc. signed a contract with the UFWOC.

The **legacy** of Cesar Chavez was what he had done for the Hispanic and immigrant population that picked America's food. Very little was known about these people, whose hard work fed the nation. Outside of the Mexican American community, the banner with Our Lady of Guadalupe was never as well known as when it appeared in grape vineyards and lettuce fields. Chavez educated Americans about the history and traditions of Latino people. He brought home how important these hard working laborers were to America's economy.

Cesar Chavez is also important as an example of a poorly educated man with no money, who followed a bold dream and found success. He educated himself and won the hearts of millions of Americans.

On August 11, 2000, California declared March 31 as a legal holiday to celebrate the birthday and life of Cesar Chavez. Earlier, Texas had made March 31 an optional state holiday in Chavez's honor. Arizona celebrated its first official Cesar Chavez day as well in 2000.

Those who followed Chavez urged Americans to make March 31 a special kind of holiday—a "day on" instead of a "day off." They urged people to celebrate Chavez's life and work. But also, to do their part in making the world a better place like he did.

In 2003 the United States Post Office issued a stamp commemorating the strength and determination of Cesar Chavez.

BIBLIOGRAPHY

Houle, Michelle, Ed. *Cesar Chavez.* San Diego: Greenhaven Press, 2003.

Matthiessen, Peter. *Sal Si Puedes.* Berkeley: University of California Press, 2000.

GLOSSARY

Anglo: a white American who is not of Hispanic descent

barrio: neighborhood in Spanish

braceros: legal workers from Mexico who do work that local people refuse to do; from brazo, meaning "arm" in Spanish

condolence: an expression of sympathy for someone who is suffering; pity

conscience: the sense of right and wrong; principles

dignity: the sense of respect for oneself

discrimination: treating a group of people differently, usually in a negative way; bias; prejudice

endorse: to show support for

fast: to stop eating for reasons of protest

legacy: that which is left behind by a person usually after his or her death

Mass: a Catholic religious celebration

mimeograph: a printing machine that makes copies of documents

mission: a place formed by a religious organization that usually provides assistance to the poor

motto: a slogan or saying for an organization

picket line: a line of people who are on strike

recruiter: a person who encourages other people to become part of a group

revolution: an uprising usually by people who want laws to be changed

rivalry: a competition between opposing groups

rundown: in a bad condition

strike: to stop working as a protest

suspicious: disbelieving, mistrustful

INDEX